The Legend of Painted Pony
and the Western Wind

A Wild Pony Book

The wind is calling —
Just Ride!

Cathy Hoffman

The Legend of Painted Pony and the Western Wind

written by **Cathy Huffman**

illustrated by **Marie Craven**

Ambassador International
GREENVILLE, SOUTH CAROLINA & BELFAST, NORTHERN IRELAND

www.ambassador-international.com

The Legend of Painted Pony and the Western Wind

ISBN: 978-1-935507-29-1

Written by Cathy Huffman
Illustrated by Marie Craven

Designed by Points & Picas
(pointsandpicas.com)

AMBASSADOR INTERNATIONAL
Emerald House
427 Wade Hampton Blvd.
Greenville, SC 29609, USA
www.ambassador-international.com

AMBASSADOR BOOKS
The Mount
2 Woodstock Link
Belfast, BT6 8DD, Northern Ireland, UK
www.ambassador-international.com

The colophon is a trademark of Ambassador

For my grandchildren who
inspire love and imagination

very year, when the sun sleeps longer and the clouds grow whiter in the blue sky, the People of the Desert remember the Painted Pony of the Superstition Mountains.

Painted Pony belonged to the great herd that roamed the desert valleys and foothills of the ancient mountains of the West.

The People of the Desert know the mountains rose from the sacred earth long before they or the ponies came to live there.

Only the horned toads and coyotes, jack rabbits and rattlesnakes, scorpions and roadrunners were keepers of the land in the ancient days.

The Old Ones say that the People of the Desert came from the far north long years before memory began.

The ponies came from the endless water in great canoes. It was the time when the buffalo still covered the prairie like a winter blanket, and the white-tailed deer were many.

Painted Pony had lived within the fences of man and had carried
him on the hunt in the desert sun and the mountain snows.
Painted Pony had seen the beginning and the end
of man, and he had loved a boy of the man herd.

The sun and moon chased each other across the sky many times, while the boy and Painted Pony raced the wind across the desert and searched the mountain for its mysteries.

Together they found hidden canyons
where the spirits go to rest; and together they
chased the wind deep into the crooked-top
mountain called Superstition.

One day they found the cave that the Western Wind calls home. But the Wind was not happy to be found, so Painted Pony took the boy and fled before the fury of the Wind.

The People of the Desert still remember the return of the boy and his pony. The People wanted to learn the secret of the Western Wind, but the secret stayed locked inside the boy. Neither the boy nor the pony ever told the secret of the Wind.

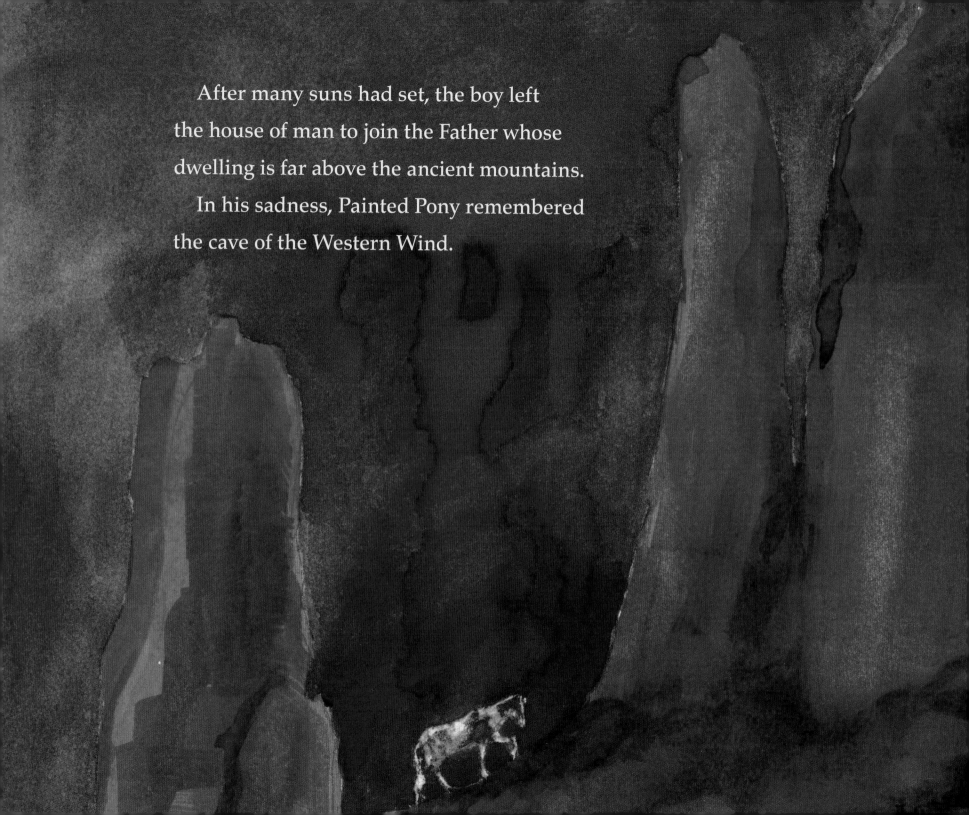

After many suns had set, the boy left
the house of man to join the Father whose
dwelling is far above the ancient mountains.
   In his sadness, Painted Pony remembered
the cave of the Western Wind.

And so it was that the People of the Desert saw Painted Pony no more.

But when the setting sun stains the clouds with pink and orange, you may see the Painted Pony gallop across the darkening sky,

And if the Western Wind is with you, you may even hear the boy's laughter—like a distant echo in your heart.

Painted Pony take your boy and fly across the sky.

Leave an evening shadow for my seeking eye.

Stir within my quiet heart secret dreams so old,

They call me to adventures mysterious and bold.

As my eyes grow weary and darkness closes in,

With stars still glowing brightly the dreaming will begin;

And I shall go a-flying, too, my mustang dark as night,

Until the wild Western Wind scatters forth new light.

About the Legend . . .

The Superstition Mountains

Superstition Mountain in the Arizona desert is a rugged, mysterious landmark. The hot summer sun can send temperatures over 115 degrees, yet winter nights can dip below freezing! Snow may fall on mountain tops and even on the desert floor. It can be a dangerous climate for those who are unprepared.

People have been fascinated by the "crooked-top" mountain since Native Americans first came to this dry, desert land. It is the legendary home of the Apaches' Thunder God, and it is also thought to be the location of the elusive Lost Dutchman gold mine. So I guess it comes as no surprise that the mountain is named—Superstition.

Desert Horned Toad (Lizard)

The horned toad is a frightful-looking lizard and not a toad at all! His threatening appearance is little more than a bluff, since he is only about 5 inches long, with a wide, flattened body. As a matter of fact, he will fit nicely into the palm of your hand.

This funny fellow hibernates in the winter and reappears when spring temperatures begin to warm. He loves basking on a rock in the sun, but if you want to catch him, he can quickly scurry away, blending into his sandy surroundings or even burying himself in the sand, where he is easily caught, since he thinks he's hiding!

Once you catch him, you can enjoy petting his soft body. The "horns" protruding above his eyes and forming a ring at the back of his head will flatten under your touch. The sharp spines that fringe his tail and sides to discourage predators are not as menacing as they look.

Not one to expend energy chasing down a delicious ant, he will simply wait until one happens by and catch it with a flick of his long, sticky, toad-like tongue.

His best defense against predators is his desert grey color. Also, markings in shades of brown, tan, black, yellow, or even a rusty red, allow him to blend in with desert plants and soils. A horned toad doesn't have many defenses, but he can inflate his body to look larger or become harder to swallow, or he may attempt scratching with his horns. His most unique defense is squirting blood from the corners of his eyes—imagine that!

Horses in North America

Now where did all our beautiful wild horses come from? Can you guess? As it turns out, Spanish explorers brought the first horses to North America in the 16th century (around the year 1540). Horses were carried across the Atlantic Ocean from Spain in sailing ships, a trip that could take a month or more. These magnificent and useful animals became an essential part of Native American life, changing forever the old ways of hunting, fighting, and traveling.

About the Author . . .

Cathy Huffman

The author was born and raised in Tucson, Arizona, where she gained a love and respect for the unique beauty of the southwest and the rich culture of Native Americans.

She now lives in the Upstate of South Carolina where she and her husband have a small farm. They grow berries and produce and care for their goats, ponies, and horses. The beauty of the land is a constant joy and inspiration.

It is her love of horses and stories that move the heart that inspired *The Legend of Painted Pony and the Western Wind.*

Learn more about Cathy and Wild Pony Books at **jewellfarmssc.com**.

About the Artist . . .

Marie Craven

The artist was born in North Carolina and spent 12 years growing up in Colorado. A 2009 graduate of Bob Jones University, Marie has a passion for art, particularly watercolor.

She currently lives at THE WILDS Christian Camp and Conference Center where she loves to spend time with children of all ages.